CLOCKWISE

• A Time-Telling Tale •

SARA PINTO

BLOOMSBURY
CHILDREN'S
BOOKS

Thomas was part of a busy, busy family.

For Aidan, Lucca, Cecilia, and William.
Oh, how the time flies.

Many thanks to my mother, Mary Hays;

my husband, Robert Mantho;

Victoria Wells Arms; and Scottie Brower

for all of their precious time.

And a special thanks to the Vermont Arts Council.

Copyright © 2006 by Sara Pinto

Typeset in Filosofia
Art created in guache
Design by Sharon Murray Jacobs

Published by Bloomsbury Publishing, New York, London, and Berlin
Distributed to the trade by Holtzbrinck Publishers

Library of Congress Cataloging-in-Publication Data
Pinto, Sara.
Clockwise / Sara Pinto.—1st U.S. ed.
p.   cm.
Summary: Thomas learns how to tell time with a new clock all his own.
ISBN-10: 1-58234-660-7 · ISBN-13: 978-1-58234-660-1 (boxed book)
ISBN-10: 1-58234-669-0 · ISBN-13: 978-1-58234-669-4 (book)
[1. Time—Fiction. 2. Clocks and watches—Fiction.] I. Title.
PZ7.P6349Cl 2006   [E]—dc22   2006040686

First U.S. Edition 2006
Printed in China

1 3 5 7 9 10 8 6 4 2

Bloomsbury Publishing, Children's Books, U.S.A.
175 Fifth Avenue, New York, NY 10010

There was always something to do or somewhere to go.

Because Thomas's family was so busy, his parents were always talking about time. But Thomas couldn't tell time. It just made him confused.

"Wake up! It's quarter after seven!"

"Do you know what time it is?"

"Hurry up and eat! It's already eight!"

Thomas decided he needed to know how to tell time.

He stared at the kitchen clock.

"What time is it?" he asked his mom.

"Eight fifteen," she answered. Thomas didn't see a fifteen on the clock.

"What time do we have to leave?" he asked.

"Eight twenty," she answered. Thomas didn't see a twenty on the clock.

Telling time is hard, thought Thomas.

The next day, while Thomas and his mother were rushing around doing errands, he saw exactly what he needed. "Stop the car!" he shouted.

When he opened the door, Thomas heard *tick, tock, tick, tock*.
"Whoa," whispered Thomas.
"May I help you?" asked the clockmaker.
"Yes," said Thomas. "I need to learn how to tell time."

"Then you've come to the right place," the clockmaker said.

"There are many different ways to learn,
but let me tell you about my favorite."

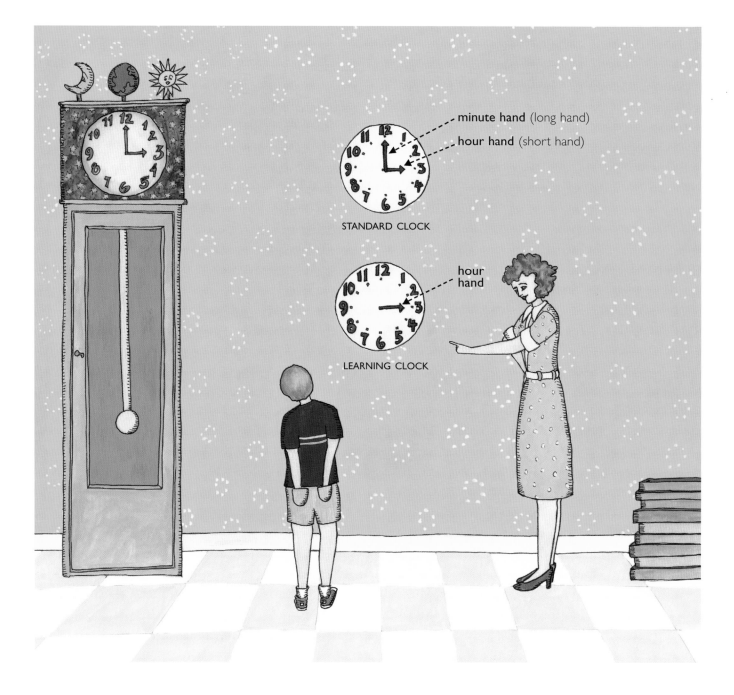

minute hand (long hand)

hour hand (short hand)

STANDARD CLOCK

hour hand

LEARNING CLOCK

"Clocks have two hands," she began. "The hands point to the numbers to tell us what time it is. The SHORT hand tells us the HOURS and the LONG hand tells us the MINUTES. The hands and the numbers work together to tell us the time."

The clockmaker pointed to a strange-looking clock on the wall.

"I think it's easiest to start with a clock that has just the hour hand on it. We start learning to tell time by telling the HOURS of the day.

When the SHORT hand points to a number, that's what HOUR it is.
Of course, the hour hand doesn't always point exactly to a number.
Sometimes it's before or after the number.
That means it's either BEFORE or AFTER that hour.

For instance, if the hour hand is BEFORE the three, it's BEFORE three o'clock.

If it's pointing EXACTLY at the three, it's EXACTLY three o'clock.

If it's pointing AFTER the three, it's AFTER three o'clock.

The hand goes all the way around, always moving in the same direction, which we call CLOCKWISE."

Just then, Thomas's mom popped her head in the door.
"Thomas dear, we're late! It's half past and the girls are done with dance class."
"Half past?" Thomas asked.

"The way people talk about time can make it very confusing," said the clockmaker. "So for now let's keep it simple. Learn the hours first. Then you can tackle the minutes."

Confusing

4:45

till

six fifteen

6:36

quarter after

a.m.

ten to

four thirty

half past

8:10

p.m.

midnight

noon

quarter of

Simple

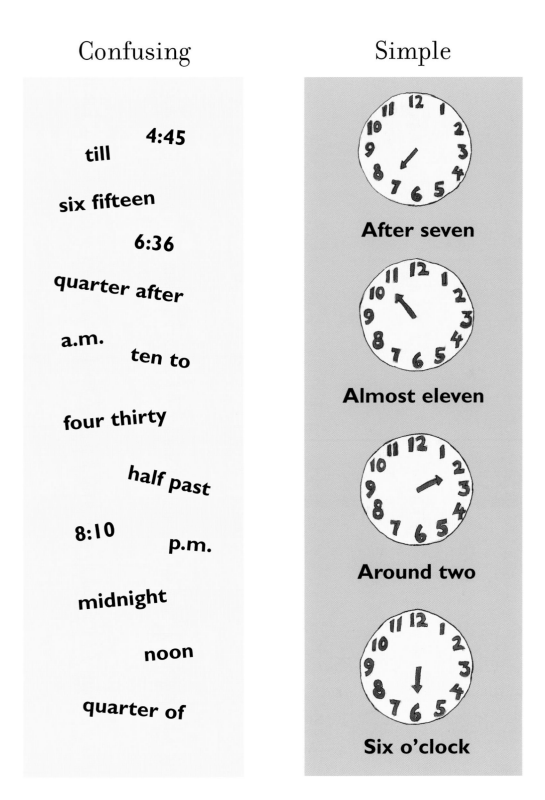

After seven

Almost eleven

Around two

Six o'clock

"Here," said the clockmaker, handing him a box.
"This is a one-handed clock you can practice with.
Add the minute hand once you understand the hours."
Thomas thanked the clockmaker and left.

That evening before bed, Thomas's mother helped him put up his clock. It was seven o'clock, so Thomas's mom moved the hour hand so it pointed exactly to the seven. Thomas looked at the hand. "It's not moving," said Thomas.

"Yes it is, honey," said his mom. "But it moves so slowly that you don't really notice it. It takes one whole hour for it to move from one number to the next."

Thomas lay in
bed, staring at the
clock. He was excited
about learning to tell time.
But soon his eyelids grew
heavy and he fell asleep.

The next morning when Thomas opened his eyes,
the first thing he did was look at his clock.
It looked like this:

Okay, thought Thomas, that must mean it's after seven.
Just then, his mother shouted up the stairs.
"Kids, it's time to get up! It's after seven!"
Oh good, thought Thomas, this is working.

Over the next few weeks, Thomas got better and better
at using his clock. Time was beginning to take shape.

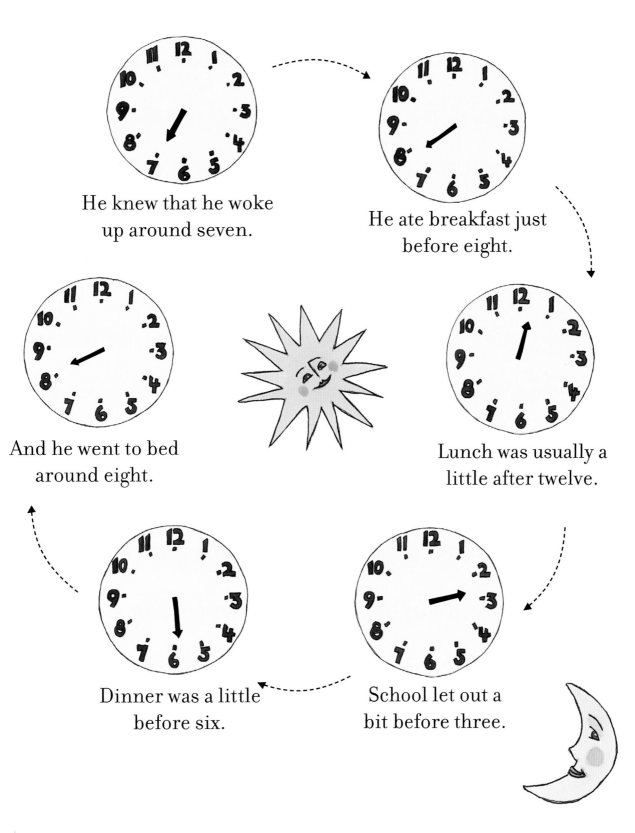

He knew that he woke
up around seven.

He ate breakfast just
before eight.

And he went to bed
around eight.

Lunch was usually a
little after twelve.

Dinner was a little
before six.

School let out a
bit before three.

Before long, Thomas was ready for minutes!

Thomas and his mother added the minute hand to his clock. "Can you count by fives up to sixty?" his mother asked.

"Sure," said Thomas. "Why?"

"Because there are SIXTY MINUTES in an HOUR. We use the hour numbers to count the minutes by fives. A new hour begins when the minute hand points to the twelve.

Let's write the minute numbers next to the hour numbers to help you remember. When the minute hand points to those numbers, that's how many minutes past the hour it is."

Thomas stared at the clock. "What are those little things between the numbers?" he asked his mom.

"Those marks help us keep track of the minutes, too," she answered. "Instead of writing all sixty numbers on the clock, there are sixty marks. There is a number for every five marks. So when the minute hand points to one of these marks, we just look at the big number closest to it. That helps us figure out the exact minute."

They practiced by moving the minute hand clockwise around the clock.

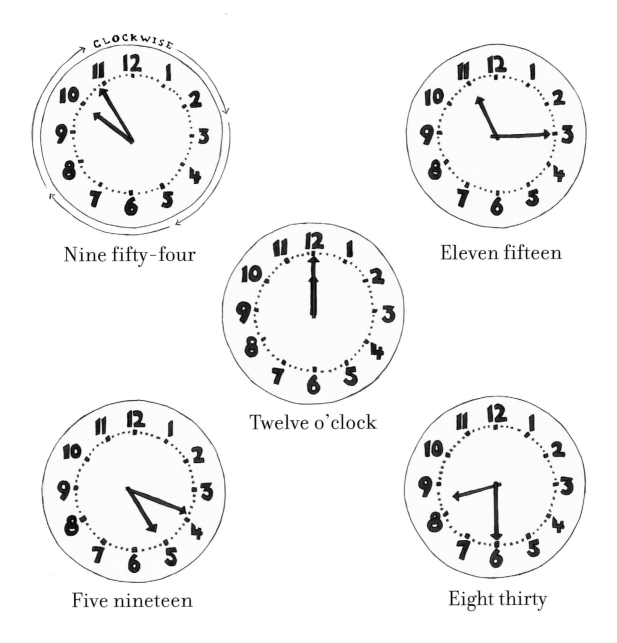

Nine fifty-four

Eleven fifteen

Twelve o'clock

Five nineteen

Eight thirty

First Thomas said the hour, then he said the minutes.
When the minute hand reached the twelve, he always said O'CLOCK.
When the minute hand reached the six, he could say it was HALF PAST
the hour, because the minute hand had gone exactly HALFWAY around
the clock. Now Thomas could keep track of minutes, too!

He figured out that if he did certain things at certain times,
he could get downstairs by seven thirty.

Up at 7:00.

7:10—Wake the girls.

7:15—Hit the bathroom.

Dressed at 7:25.

Downstairs by 7:30.

Thomas loved the feeling
that telling time gave him.
Master of his own destiny!
Commander of his own ship!
On time for breakfast!

Thomas's family was still a busy one, but now Thomas had time on his side. And that was a great feeling.